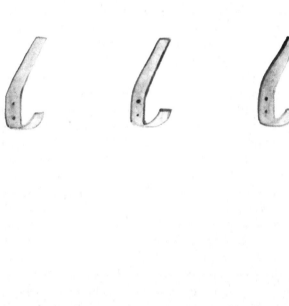

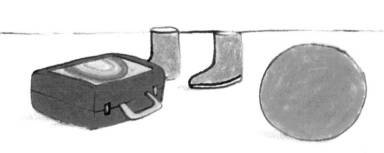

For Kit
xxx

Thank you to Hannah, Jo, Louise, Sam, Sorrel,
Mum, Richard and most of all, Kit.

First published 2019 by Macmillan Children's Books
This edition published 2020 by Macmillan Children's Books
an imprint of Pan Macmillan
The Smithson, 6 Briset Street, London ECIM 5NR
Associated companies throughout the world
www.panmacmillan.com

ISBN: 978-1-4472-5052-4

Text and illustrations copyright © Rebecca Cobb 2019, 2020

The right of Rebecca Cobb to be identified as the author and illustrator
of this work has been asserted by her in accordance with the
Copyright, Designs and Patents Act 1988.

3 5 7 9 8 6 4 2

A CIP catalogue record for this book is available from the British Library.

Printed in China.

# Hello, Friend!

Rebecca Cobb

MACMILLAN CHILDREN'S BOOKS

I love to play with my friend.

Hello, friend!

We play
all sorts
of things.

We love to
jump around,

and go fast
on the bike.

I show my friend how to build
tall towers. He's doing very well.

I'm really good at sharing . . .

especially at lunchtimes.

And I'm extra
helpful when we
put our coats on.

We're so excited
to go outside!

We would stay out all
day long if we could.

Sometimes we
do quiet things,

and sometimes we do noisy things.

Other times we do nothing at all.

I'm always sad when it's time to go home,

because I will miss my friend.

I hope he misses me?

I think he might!

And even though I don't like
to say goodbye, I can't wait
until tomorrow . . .

because I'm looking forward
to all the fun we can have . . .

together.

I really love to play with my friend,
and my friend loves to play with me.

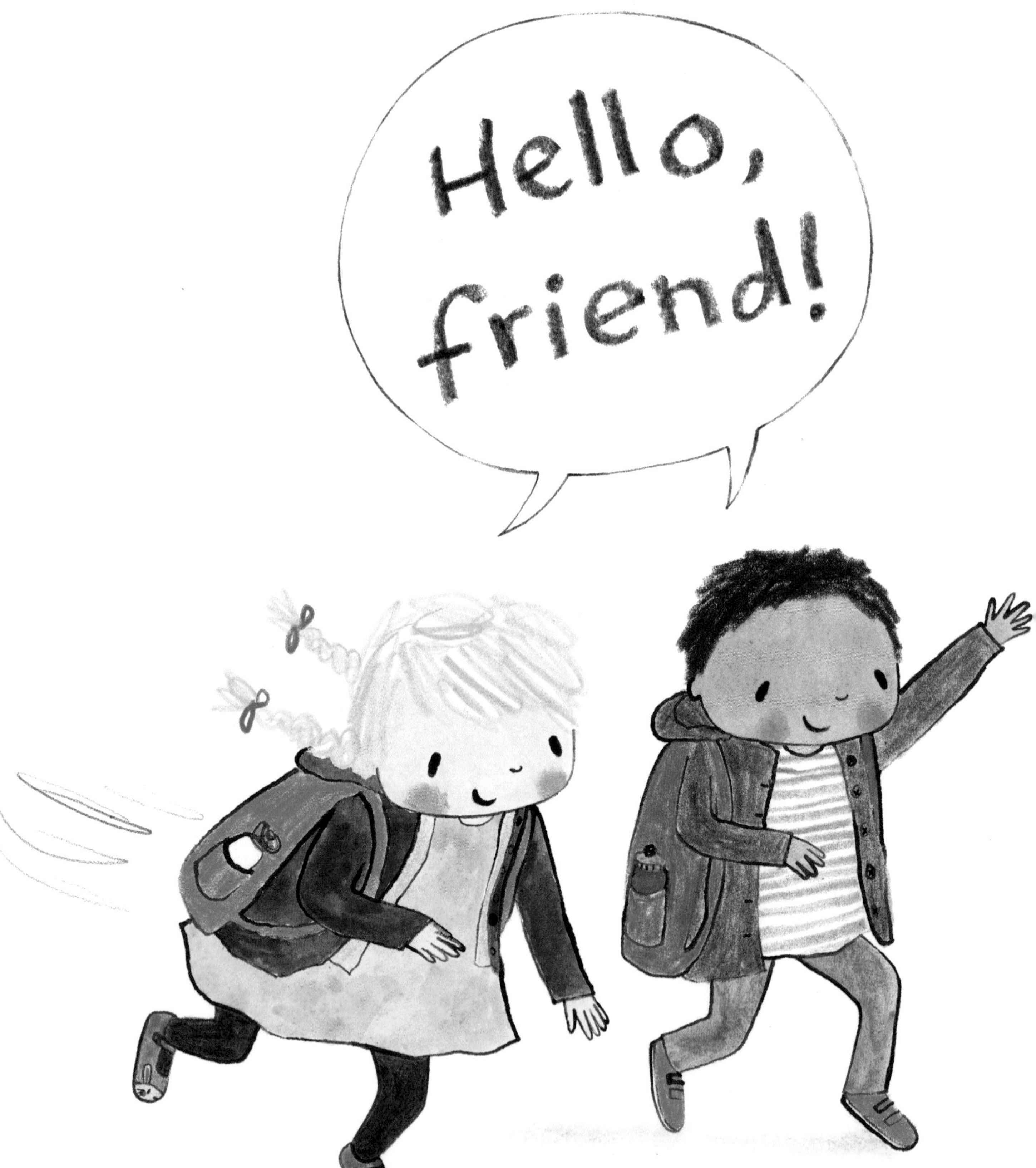
Hello, friend!

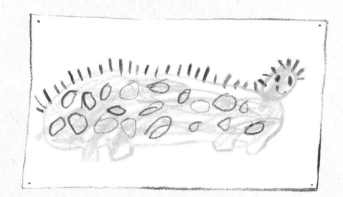

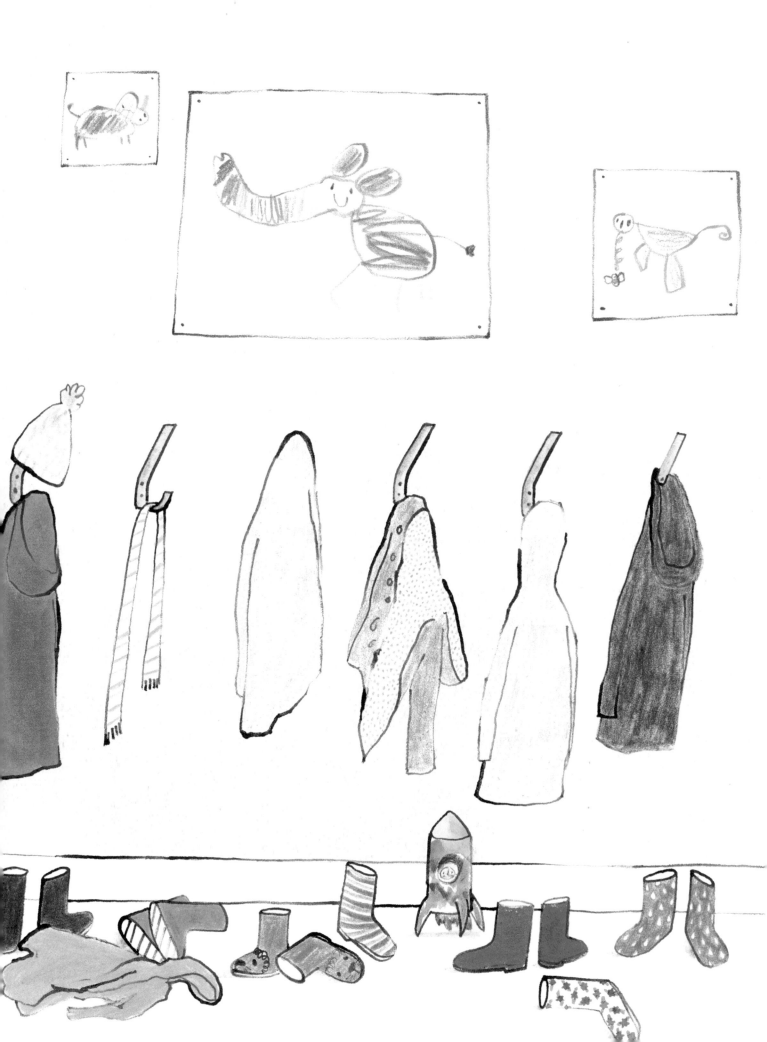